TONIGHT'S SPECIALS

Five Stories. One Vietnamese Restaurant.

MINA ALLAN   G. J. CRESPO   WENDY M. MCDONALD

MEGAN M. MULLIN   PHOEBE SINCLAIR

Foreword by
ANNETTE TROSSELLO

Table
for 7

Published by Table for 7 Press

ISBN: 978-1-7369254-8-5 (paperback); 978-1-7369254-9-2 (ebook)

This is a work of fiction. Names, characters, places, and events are solely the product of the author's imagination and/or are used fictitiously. Any resemblance to actual persons, living or dead, or to places, businesses, companies, events, or locales is entirely coincidental.

Summary: Five authors from Table for Seven Press weave together short stories that explore the eternal question: "What if…?" when the promise of tickets to see a beloved band are on the horizon.

[1. diverse characters 2. mystery 3. humor 4. ghosts 5. first date 6. new adult 7. interconnected]

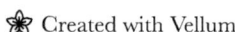 Created with Vellum

To all the noodle houses, diners,

and ice cream shoppes

that have fed our creativity over the years

Contents

Foreword

Writers

What Society Thinks We Do: Sit alone at a mahogany desk in a dark room writing the next great American novel.

What My Friends Think We Do: Bang out flawless first drafts while sipping espresso at the local coffee shop.

What We Actually Do: Write and rewrite, procrastinate, outline on notecards, pick up errant cats off notecards, plot and replot, knit and brainstorm, bike and brainstorm, commute and brainstorm, procrastinate, write and rewrite, and (perhaps most importantly) meet with our fellow writers in critique groups.

Some think of writing as a solitary endeavor, but it is a social art. Every writer needs a trusted friend, someone who can be an early reader, offer advice on character arcs, and point out plot holes. And if you are as lucky as I am, you may end up with a whole group of writer friends.

Back in 2008, I joined a critique group and found fellow storytellers who helped inspire and lift each other up. We are a fun and diverse crew with a range of interests: reading, writing, *Star Wars*, banned books, fantasy books, Avengers, Sci-fi movies, fanfiction, rom-coms, board games, biking, and paddle boarding to name a few. We daylight in a school library, publishing company, college of art, home office, travel company, and nonprofit. We've met for dinners, lunches, and retreats. We've read dozens of drafts of each other's works. It was only a matter of time before we decided we wanted to take our collaboration to the next level and create a book together—that is how *Tonight's Special* was born.

The short stories in this collection are set at our favorite Boston-area Vietnamese restaurant. While there is some overlap, with characters passing each other—and sometimes interacting—each story stands on its own. The stories center on various parties meeting up for dinner before a concert. A fictional band, the Styrofoam Rockets originated in Phoebe Sinclair's as-of-yet unpublished YA novel and migrated to Erin Dionne's middle grade book, *Secrets of a Fangirl*. The band next had a cameo in Gary Crespo's young adult novel, *How to Ruin Your Life in 140 Characters or Less*. Readers of *Tonight's Special* will hopefully enjoy spotting this popular band that eludes exact description in five stories.

While I was on hiatus from Table for Seven Press as I completed my M.Ed. in Library Media and started a new career as a Library Media Specialist, my fellow writers completed this amazing book. I was honored to be asked to write this foreword and to help with some finishing touches. We hope you have as much fun reading this anthology as we did creating it.

Annette Trossello

15 Year Critique Group Member

Gaby & Flor &

Phoebe Sinclair

"YOU REALLY THINK you're gonna need that?" Flor asked, watching her friend pull on a sweatshirt.

Instead of responding, Gaby countered with a question of her own, "How long do you think it will take to get there?"

They were posted in Gaby's dorm, which was a big, white, over-bright cube comprised of cinderblocks, jammed with the belongings of three-too-many young women. *Not a speck of wall in sight,* Gaby liked to complain.

This didn't mean much to Flor, who'd grown up in a narrow brownstone, about which she complained, was *all brown, brown, brown, stone, stone, stone.* Her childhood equally refused tacks, tape, and that sticky blue goo that claimed easy removal but left paper smudged with grease.

"Sweatshirt?" Flor tried again.

Gaby shot her a flat stare; Flor proved impervious. They'd known one another too long. From their rambunctious, giggly middle school years, to being one another's confidant and occasional competitor at the exam high school they'd both tested into, along with their close buddy, Dean. Now, as second-year college students, there wasn't a smile, frown, or side-eye exchanged between the two of them that the other couldn't cheerfully deflect or parry right damn back.

"Yes, yes, yes," Flor ducked to zip up her boots. "It's New England. I know. But also, that's *my* sweatshirt you just put on."

"Your point?" Gaby checked out her reflection in a mirror that itself was barely visible between the many hoodies, scarves, and strands of jewelry that hung from a row of back-of-door hooks. She blew at the straight strands dangling past her nose and considered black eyelashes that accepted mascara but resisted metal curlers. Gaby had grown two full inches since high school while retaining a trim, athletic build.

For her part, Flor tried not to feel too many kinds-of-way about her now-curvier-curves, curls, and fashion sense that maybe occasionally embarrassed her Abuelita. ("Unconventional," her mom called it.)

Gaby continued to grouse, "It's not like you haven't borrowed all of my good jackets and have them lining that squirrel's nest that you call a single, right? Anyway, you're wearing boots. Should I be wearing boots? Is it gonna be a boots kind of show?"

"How would I know?" Flor asked, straightening. "This will be my first time going to the venue. Unlike some *other people*, I haven't had a fake ID that gets me into the clubs I shouldn't be at."

"Hey!" Gaby protested with a rueful grin. "Not every place is all-ages. Also, you haven't addressed *my* question. Fine. Guess I'll answer it myself."

Flor watched Gaby flop down on her roommate's bed instead of her own because *bad boundaries* and pull out her phone, talking all the while. "Okay. The restaurant where we're meeting your new friends is in Brookline, right? Then the club is in Fenway. We could walk. It's a nice night."

Flor folded herself onto the bed beside Gaby, knee-first, peering over her shoulder at the glossy screen, "We should take the C line to Coolidge Corner, where the Vietnamese place is. Then I guess we could walk from there, if there's time."

"You don't show up for concerts on time, Flor." Gaby turned her head, setting her intense gaze on Flor's face. They were sitting so close that Flor imagined Gaby saw mostly a sweep of dark curls and her distinctive nose that Flor once vowed to 'fix' through the magic of plastic surgery. As teens, Gaby and Flor often confided what they would change about themselves—for Gaby an exhausting ambiguity that led her to play up features inherited from either her Taiwanese dad or her Boston Irish mom one day, only to downplay them the next; for Flor that nose, or even her raspy voice, passed through generations of Dominican women. (Whenever he heard them at it, Dean couldn't resist adding something like, "You're complaining. If I didn't dye my hair pink, I'd fade into these egg white walls." Easy for *him* to say.)

"I guess not." Flor said, thinking wistfully of their friend's dry observations, and also his weird obsession with being on time that had provided excellent cover for Flor's smidge of social anxiety.

"Hey," Gaby leaned even closer. "Something the matter? You seem awfully keyed up about dinner and a show. It's eighteen-plus. Not like you need an ID for that."

Flor shrugged, dropping her eyes to her hands, which had moved to grip one another in her lap. "I just want everything to work out okay. And these are new... friends. I wanna make a good impression. You know I'm not good at that."

"What? Who says?"

Flor couldn't help the dry laugh that came out, "Um, YOU. Everyone."

Gaby threw her arms around Flor so that they were sitting in a slightly awkward position with Flor facing forward, looking across the dorm room towards Gaby's riotously messy bed, and Gaby so close that her details blurred—her blue-tipped black hair, the dark freckles across her forehead and nose, those enviable cheekbones.

"You're doing it again," Gaby accused.

"I'm not doing anything! What?"

"You're thinking these people—your new, strange Internet buddies—don't *really* want you around. You think they're putting up with you. Which is ridiculous."

Flor pulled back. Gaby hung on a little tighter before relenting, letting her arms drop. There were a few downsides to having known one another for so long. This was one.

"I never said that."

"You didn't have to. I know you. I know how you are."

"Yeah, well, you don't know *these* people yet. And it's not just college kids like us, it's a mixed group. Like, there'll be grown-ups."

"Flor," Gaby said seriously. "Do you want to sit around here and fret, or do you want to see for real how it's going to be instead of making up more and more reasons not to go?"

"Ugh!" Flor stood up and headed towards the door. "Gaby, you're so annoying."

Even with her back turned, Flor guessed at her friend's knowing smirk.

How would things be different if she had gone to college in a different city? Flor watched her and Gaby's shadows slanting across the sidewalk as they exited the dorm, crossed out of Simmons University territory, and wove through clusters of undergrad students on their trek to the nearest Green Line station. For once, time was on their side; no need to walk at a shin-breaking speed. The city rolled past, worn and familiar and theirs. Tall brick buildings topped with turrets and spirals sat in seeming communion with new steel and glass sky-scraping luxury housing. Too-big-for-a-city SUVs stopped, brakes squeaking, on the very edge of the crosswalk, forcing pedestrians to skirt front bumpers and throw grumpy glares over their shoulders. As they passed the Muddy River, squirrels darted nervously, contrasting with the slow-moving clouds of Canada geese that waddled and plucked at manicured greenery.

Other cities had a mix of old and new architecture. Other cities offered pockets of green. Other cities had trolleys like the Green Line train that they'd boarded, tapping their student cards against the reader and nodding vaguely at the unsmiling driver. In other cities, students crammed together with families and office workers and grandparents stoically outnumbered by toddlers left in their care by harried young professionals. In Boston, shops and bakeries and banks rolled quickly by as Flor and Gaby hung onto the vinyl straps and peered over the traffic at bubble tea shops they'd try as soon as their work study checks came in. As they pointed and chatted, Flor felt the itchiness recede —that feeling of nothing being right, not knowing, wanting to just stay where she was and avoid the awkwardness and uncertainty.

Flor had expected things would get easier as she aged. Not so. Somehow, knowing more hadn't eased her feeling of ill-ease. With her grades, her high school's reputation, and her professor aunt's facility with financial aid, she'd had the pick among the colleges she'd applied to. Going clear across the country had had its appeal, but then there was Gaby at Simmons and Dean at Harvard, (then dropped out of Harvard), and her parents in Rozzie and her little sister, still in high school. Now, two years in, Flor could admit to herself that she hadn't been ready to leave.

"Next stop, Coolidge Corner," called the recorded voice.

Gaby elbowed her unnecessarily. "Head out of the clouds, star baby."

As they descended to the sidewalk, her friend kept close and, on a whim, Flor took her hand. Gaby smiled, surprised. Crossing with the crowd of commuters, they took off running, unnecessarily. Hand-in-hand, they raced down the sidewalk, giggling as they avoided other pedestrians and narrowly missed colliding with a bicycle at the corner of Harvard and Longwood. They were both puffing as they skidded to a halt at the end of the block.

"I think we passed the restaurant," Gaby said. "It's back this way."

They retraced their steps and Flor felt some of her energy burst ebb away. She paused with her hand on the door.

"Want me to go in first?" Gaby offered.

Flor drew in a deep breath. "No. That's okay."

In the vestibule, a large fish tank bubbled away.

"Whoa," said Gaby. "Check out the size of those goldfish!"

Through the next door was the restaurant proper. It wasn't one they'd yet experienced, although Flor recognized it as one she'd passed many times during her years of hanging out downtown Brookline as a teen. Places like this one were what adults chose when they went out together.

Directly inside, an older woman greeted them at the hostess stand. Flor eyed the wooden statue that sat beside an ornate bowl filled with peppermints. Off to the left was a full bar with stools. At the very top of the bar, facing the window, she spotted several Maneki-neko cats waving their paws placidly at the world. Ahead of them and to the right, the dining room held a number of large and small tables. The dinner crowd hadn't yet arrived, it appeared, as only a few tables held diners. Flor scanned for anyone she knew, and there they were—the group they'd come to meet.

A handsome guy with hair braided in plaits grinned. He stood and waved.

"Flor! We're over here."

"Wow," Gaby whispered. "You did not mention HIM."

Flor shushed her, received an elbow-to-the-ribs in response, and waved, trying to feel more assured than she did. She glanced at the hostess, who nodded bland assent, and led the way to the large, round, lacquered wood table filled with college-age people, and a few slightly older. Seeing so many people she didn't really know looking at them expectantly, Flor wanted to turn around and run away. She shoved that feeling down, held her ground and said, "Hi."

"Hi!" the group chorused back.

"Glad you could make it Flor," the guy—Xander, she knew from the online fan forum where they'd met and had been chatting enthusiastically since they were both first-year students. He left his seat and stood at the edge of the group. Shorter, stockier, and more built than she'd expected, he beamed at her, friendliness pouring off in waves. "I'm so excited to finally meet in person! You okay with a hug? I don't wanna be weird."

"Um, no, sure, that's fine." Before Flor could blink, Xander encased her and squeezed. It was an amazing hug. Warmth rippled up her spine. She attempted to offer something in return and lamely patted his back as he moved to step away. Her sense of ease plummeted, but the grin didn't leave his face as Xander returned to his seat.

"Uh," Flor started, and then wasn't sure what to say next. Beside her, Gaby cleared her throat theatrically.

"Sorry!" Flor said, "This is Gaby. We've been friends since we were kids. Gaby, this is Xander and, um, lots of people whose names I don't… actually know."

"Well, that's unexpected," said Gaby easily, without missing a beat. "But I'm down."

Xander laughed. "How it goes when you make friends online! Grab a seat. We haven't ordered yet."

Once Flor and Gaby had squeezed in, making them a table of seven, Xander went around with perfect, enviable confidence, introducing everyone by name and pseudonym. Flor nodded and smiled along, each name flying from her mind the second it landed.

"Need any recommendations?" asked the girl across from Gaby. "We come here all the time because we're all obsessed with phở."

"That's soup, right?" Flor said, hesitantly.

Beside her, Gaby jerked oddly in her seat, causing Flor to look up.

"Dean?" said Gaby.

And there he was, in all his pink haired glory: Dean, whom they hadn't heard much from since the summer when he announced his plan to take a year (or more) off from college (Harvard!). He wore an apron around his waist and held a notepad and pen, seeming just as surprised to see them as they were to see him.

"Uh, hey guys," he said.

For a moment, there was silence as everyone processed. Then Gaby shot out of her chair, and Flor followed. Dean's expression had gone from surprised to carefully neutral, but of course, they would have none of that. The three met in a laughing embrace before Gaby and Flor backed off.

"You *work* here?" Gaby said.

"It's been forever!" Flor lightly slapped his arm. "Why didn't you tell us you got a job at a restaurant?"

Dean shrugged. "Sorry, there's just been a lot going on."

Gaby glanced around, "You must be like the only white boy working here?"

"Almost,"

"We're going to the Styrofoam Rockets concert after dinner. Do you want to come? We haven't hung out in forever."

"Not sure my shift will be over in time," Dean hesitated, looking across the restaurant at what was probably his bosses wondering why he hadn't taken orders yet. "…and I don't have a ticket."

"We've got an extra," Xander said, smiling up at their reunion. "You can have it. No need to pay us back."

"Oh no," Dean frowned. "I couldn't do that—"

"Seriously," Xander interrupted. "Please take it. We were just going to give it to the first person we saw outside the club who didn't have one."

"All of you are going?" Dean asked.

Around the table, heads nodded. When he seemed confused, Xander explained, "We run a music fanzine. Like all of us together. We go to shows and interview local musicians, and there are some other features, too, like stuff about skateboarding and doing cool things in the city."

"It's print, but we also have the zine posted online," another person at the table added.

"I'll write the website on the back of the ticket," Xander offered, and sat down to do that.

Flor and Gaby took their seats as well. Dean, of course, couldn't join them directly, but he treated their table to a few extra appetizers.

The meal was fun and easy. Flor could hardly believe her luck in making this connection with so many cool people. Gaby, textbook extrovert that she was, chatted everyone up, letting Flor be mostly quiet, but not uncomfortably so. When it was time to settle up and leave, Xander slid a printed-out concert ticket across the table to Flor. His expression was so earnest and open, Flor struggled to not falter in taking it.

"Here," Xander said. "I think if you give this to your friend, he'll be more likely to accept it."

"That's probably true," Gaby nodded.

As they prepared to leave, Flor and Gaby hung back. Dean came to collect payment, and Flor handed over the ticket.

"I really can't," he said, but Gaby waved him off.

"Even if you can't come to the show," Flor said. "We want to see you. Let's make a plan, ok?"

Dean hesitated, prompting Gaby to do her usual. She grabbed his arm, yanking him towards her so that she could press her cold nose against his cheek. "Say yes, SAY YES!"

Laughing, Dean fought her off. "Okay, okay."

"Yeah?" Flor looked him in the eye, trying for stern.

"Yeah," he nodded. "Your friends are waiting."

"We're waiting TOO, Dean," Gaby reached for him again, but Flor caught her by the arm and started dragging her towards the door.

"See you soon?"

"Sure."

When she glanced back, Flor caught something in Dean's expression that made her blooming smile falter and fade as Gaby's bouncy momentum carried them out the door.

Ticket Turmoil

Mina Allan

"YOU ARE A FREAKING *DISASTER*!" Andrea Biscotti shouted. She slammed a fist on the horn and a foot on the brake. Her tiny Honda bleated, echoing her displeasure. The red Mazda that cut her off finished making its left turn, its driver cheerfully throwing the finger out the window.

"Road rage much, Auntie?" Her twelve-year-old niece, Beatrice, glanced up from her phone.

"Only in Massachusetts." Andrea got through the traffic light, bumping over the train tracks and making the left turn onto Harvard Ave, sweat breaking out under her arms. Pedestrians wove in and out of traffic without fear. She was pretty sure she'd have a nervous breakdown before she found parking.

Her friend Boo had suggested the Vietnamese place for dinner, explaining that she could park in Brookline and she and Beatrice could either walk or take the T into Boston when they were done. At this point, Andrea was ready to ditch the car, the dinner, *and* the surprise concert she was bringing Beatrice to, and hop an Amtrak back to south county, Rhode Island, where she belonged.

"I'm *starving*," Bea whined.

"You should've had a snack before we left," Andrea said through clenched teeth. She scanned the street for an available parking spot. Her GPS said the restaurant was .1 miles away, but that felt like ten miles with the traffic gridlock.

"I wasn't hunnngry then." Bea drew the word out. Andrea had made them leave plenty early, but they still hit a ton of traffic, and her dramatic niece was known to get hangry.

Just like me, she thought with a laugh.

Ahead, a Prius pulled out of a spot. Andrea threw her blinker on and offered a prayer to the parking gods.

Please let me get this spot before I murder my niece and Madison Beech.

The whole thing was Madison's fault.

Madison Beech, pop icon and Andrea's friend and neighbor in Beach Hill, Rhode Island, found out that Andrea's niece was obsessed with the band Styrofoam Rockets.

"No *way!*" she cried. "The bass player did some session work for me during quarantine. Let me get you passes to their Boston show. You'll be the best auntie ever!"

"They're all she talks about and I've never even listened to their stuff," Andrea admitted. "I'm not sure I'm the best—"

"Done!" Madison held up her phone.

> Tix & passes for 2 in Boston? Friend & niece.

Done x 2

came the response thirty minutes later.

Andrea shook her head. Madison's reach was pretty far, and although she appreciated the perks of having a famous friend, sometimes the gulf between them was so wide. The concert had been sold out for months, and the closer the concert date, the mopier Bea became. Andrea would be Auntie of the Year for sure... but what was she getting into?

"I'd go with you, but I'm going to Ibiza that week for a photo shoot," Madison sipped her cucumber-infused water.

Of course.

Now, as she made her sixth attempt to parallel park her Honda between a Tesla and a giant pickup truck in aggressive Brookline traffic, she cursed every Ibiza-related bone in Madison's body.

Ultimately, three people helped guide her into the spot.

Face flaming, shirt sticking to her back, Andrea finally turned off the ignition, preparing to take a deep breath.

"Let's *go!*" Bea cried, throwing open the passenger side door—thank goodness it was the one closest to the sidewalk, because Andrea didn't want to explain a pancaked child to her brother—and bouncing on her toes on the sidewalk.

"Simmer down, gunpowder!" Andrea clambered from the car, squeezing as tight as she could against the open door to avoid the bicycles, cars, and the lone electric scooter that zipped by. Beach Hill had plenty of summer traffic, but Front Street was one lane in each direction, the locals never parked downtown, and Andrea used her scooter, Daisy, almost exclusively from late May to October. It seemed like everyone in the greater Boston area was trying to get down Harvard Ave right now.

At the meter, she fumbled for change, then realized it used some sort of fancy app. "Of course," she muttered. Downloaded, linked, added enough money to ensure they were good til at least ten pm. They wouldn't need to be here any later than that, would they? On her phone screen, The Wheel of Waiting spun as the app processed her request.

"Auntie! Check out the clock tower! Auntie, did you see the size of that ice cream cone? That puppy is sooo cute!" Bea took pictures of everything she pointed out. Her niece wanted to be a photographer someday. Andrea smiled and nodded at the barrage of observations and gritted her teeth. *A snack. I need a snack, and then I will appreciate our "adventure" more.*

The app dinged, confirming their parking. "All set!" Andrea said with forced joy. "Let's eat."

Luckily, the restaurant was only a couple of doors down. Bea spotted the blue awning first, and fairly pulled Andrea the last twenty feet towards it. A couple, clearly on a date —their first?—stood in front of the hostess station.

"Whoa. Look at the size of those goldfish!" Bea said, pointing. Andrea turned, preparing to roll her eyes, but was, in fact, surprised by the size of the fish. Were they okay in that little tank?

As they waited, a salt-and-pepper haired gentleman wearing a dark jacket carrying a book, folder, and disordered pile of papers squeezed past on his way out of the restaurant. The corner of the folder caught on the door, knocking everything out of his hands. Papers littered the ground.

The man swore under his breath.

"I'll help!" Bea said. She scrambled across the floor, grabbing papers and handing them back to the guy, who Andrea guessed was some sort of professor at one of Boston's many colleges.

The door closed behind him.

"I can't find my ticket!"

The voice coming from the dining room was so loud that everyone paused and turned to the young woman in a blue hoodie. She sat at a table with two friends, hands in her hair.

"My ticket! It's *gone*!" she cried.

"Have you checked your purse?" one of the women at the table asked in a lower voice, clearly uncomfortable with her friend's display.

The upset woman raised a small clutch. "It barely fits in here."

"I told you that a paper ticket was a bad idea," their dining companion said with an eye roll. She went back to tapping on her phone with long, perfectly manicured aqua nails.

"I know, but the battery life on my phone sucks. No way am I missing Styrofoam Rockets because my stupid phone died, so my mom told me to print it." A stricken expression crossed her face. "But if I can't find that ticket, I can't go!"

A sharp poke in the side pulled Andrea away from the drama unfolding at the table. Bea glanced up at her. "We have to help her," she whispered.

"What? How?"

The hostess, holding two menus, gestured to Andrea. "I can seat you now."

Andrea followed the woman to a table for two against a far wall, diagonally across from the ticket drama table.

Bea plopped into her chair.

"We have to help," she said. "Did you hear? That ticket is for *Styrofoam Rockets*! She won't be able to go to the concert if she can't find it!"

Andrea glanced at the three women. The one with the missing ticket had dumped the contents of her small hot pink clutch on the table and was pawing through them. Her two friends exchanged tight-lipped glances over her head. "Hot. Mess," the one with the nails mouthed to the other.

"I don't know what we can do, honey," Andrea said, opening her menu. "She's looking. Maybe she left it at home. Or it'll probably turn up in her bag. Or pockets," she added, as the woman stood, patting herself down and checking her jeans.

"You have to help," Bea said firmly. "Her friends aren't doing anything, and you've solved tons of mysteries."

...*but those involve dead bodies, not lost tickets,* Andrea wanted to say. *And I usually eat dinner first.*

She pulled her eyes away from the noodle dish descriptions. Both of the woman's companions were pretend-focusing on their phones while their friend seemed more and more frazzled.

"Fine," Andrea sighed. "Order some spring rolls or something if the waitress comes over." She pushed away from the table.

I love my niece. I love my niece, she repeated as she crossed the restaurant. Bea had a big heart and was always ready to help Andrea at Biscotti Realty. She stacked brochures, packed the welcome baskets for the summer guests, and attacked the sometimes-sticky toy box with antibacterial wipes once a week. That was one of the reasons why Andrea was bringing her to the concert. It was just as much a thank you for her work as it was an auntie-niece bonding moment.

"Hi," Andrea said. She stood awkwardly in the middle of the restaurant, hovering at the lost ticket holder's elbow. "My niece and I heard about your lost ticket," Andrea pointed, and the woman turned to spot Bea, who gave a cheerful wave, "and I wanted to see if I could help you look?" Heat flamed in her cheeks.

I love my niece. I love my niece.

"Oh, that is so nice of you! I'm just so upset. I can't imagine where it went."

"Paper can go anywhere," her friend pointed out. "That's why we don't use it."

"Um, did you look under the placemats?" Andrea offered. Clearly, these friends were no help.

"I'm Quinny," the woman said. "And that's Isabelle and Chloe." Chloe had the nails. Together, Andrea and Quinny moved dishes and peered at the sticky dribbles of peanut sauce on the table. No ticket. Andrea's stomach rumbled.

Andrea really hoped this would satisfy Bea, but her mouth and brain were clearly on different programs. She heard herself say, "Where did you last have it?"

But before anyone could answer, the sharp clatter of cutlery against dishes cut through the restaurant. Andrea turned to see what caused the commotion. An elderly man at a table across the restaurant was poised rigidly in his chair, eyes wide, face an alarming color of red. He swiped his hand across the tabletop, sending a water glass and bottle of beer flying.

"He's choking!"

Andrea didn't know where the shout came from. The older woman sitting across from the gentleman sat frozen. It seemed the rest of the diners were, too.

"Someone help him!"

The waitstaff snapped off excited words in Vietnamese, but it was as though time slowed. A pink-haired busboy plunked his bucket of dirty dishes on the table he was cleaning. The man's face darkened.

The pink-haired kid—couldn't have been more than early college age—raced to the table in four big strides. His white busboy uniform was smeared with sauces and stains.

He leaned down to the gentleman's face. "I am going to help you!" he shouted. He didn't wait for any signal or response, just grabbed the man under the arms and heaved him out of the booth.

Somehow, he managed to slip around behind the guy without dropping him.

"HAH!" The noise that came out of the kid was somewhere between a grunt and a shout as he jerked hard into the man's solar plexus. The man bent forward. Nothing happened.

"HEE-YAH!" the kid shouted again. Another jerk.

This time, the guy went stock still, and a partially chewed shrimp flew from his mouth and splatted on the blue-carpeted floor. The man retched, gasped, and his face went from purple to red.

The busboy let go of the man, who sank to the edge of the booth. His dining companion went to his side, and the restaurant burst into applause for the busboy, who flushed nearly as red as his choking victim.

Could this day get any more dramatic? Andrea thought.

"Wow," Isabelle said, bringing Andrea's attention back to their table. "This dinner is not what I was expecting."

"Me either," Quinny responded. "And if I don't find my ticket, there is going to be another tragedy tonight!"

"Maybe it fell on the floor?" Andrea asked, one eye on the choking victim, who still seemed woozy. The busboy, who was probably shaken up from his heroics, was nowhere to be found.

"I know I had it when we sat down," said Quinny. "I remember folding it to keep it out of the way of the food, and I—oh!—yes! I remember! I stuck it in my back pocket!"

"Maybe it fell on the floor?" Andrea said again. The chair backs were open.

"Maybe. Can you look over there?"

"Sure," Andrea said. *How do I always end up in these situations?* She glanced at Isabelle and Chloe, who were sort-of bending to look under the table. *That's how. Some friends* they *are.*

She crouched low, scanning the blue-carpeted floor: People's shoes and crusty bits of food that the carpet sweeper would pick up later; no ticket. She purposely avoided looking in the direction of the choker, as she didn't want to lose what was left of her appetite. "Nothing," she said. She straightened, knees popping.

"I don't know what could've happened to it," Andrea said.

Quinny the ticket owner also stood, and Andrea was surprised to find that the girl was considerably taller than she. "I mean, it clearly fell off the chair," *where you really shouldn't have tucked a ticket that gets you into the concert you're so obsessed over*, she thought but didn't say out loud, "I'm really sorry."

The girl's eyes went glassy with tears. She tugged her hoodie's string. "Thanks for helping me look. These two—" she gestured with her thumb— "are acting like it's no big deal. But it *is*." She frowned.

"I know." Andrea glanced at Bea, hoping her niece wasn't traumatized by the choking. Bea was sitting in front of a plate of spring rolls, happily chowing down. She gave them a wave. Andrea's stomach growled again.

"Hey, I should let you eat," Quinny said. "Thanks for your help."

"What are you going to do about the concert?"

Quinny shrugged. "I think the digital tickets disappear when you print out a hard copy, but I do have my receipt. And I'm sitting with them. So maybe the box office can help me?"

That sounded like a lot of work and the potential for a bad outcome, but Andrea wasn't going to say that to her. "Good luck," she offered, and turned back to her table.

As she slid into her seat across from Bea, something nagged at the back of her mind.

"Didn't find it, huh?" Bea asked. She stuffed the last piece of spring roll into her mouth.

Andrea shook her head, wishing she'd told Bea to save a piece for her. "No luck," she said. "But I was thinking…"

"About the guy who dropped all those papers?" Bea asked. "Me too."

"If he'd had them stacked on the floor or something… Maybe he could've…?"

Bea nodded. "That's what must have happened. See if you can find him?"

Andrea put her head in her hands and rubbed her eyes. She was starving, cranky, didn't want to spend her time helping this woman find her ticket, but also wanted to be a good role model for her niece.

"Bea, maybe we just tell her to go look for him? I mean, this *is* a city and he's probably long gone by now!"

"Yeah, but she probably didn't even pay attention to him. *You* saw him. *I* saw him. He had all those papers. What if he's out there," she gestured towards the window, "and we miss our chance?

"I'll order some pad thai for you, Auntie. Go look. Just really quick. Then we can let it go, ok? And don't tell her —just in case nothing happens. I'll be fine right here."

Just in case nothing happens, Andrea grumbled to herself. *More like, 'nothing is going to happen and I'm wasting my time.'* But by the time she finished her grouchy thought, she was passing the fish tank again and headed out to Harvard Ave.

There were just as many people walking, driving, laughing, biking, and scooting as when they arrived at the restaurant —she glanced at the display on her phone—fifteen minutes ago. *Had it only been fifteen minutes? Really?*

Andrea shook her head. She scanned the sidewalk in both directions. Although she didn't know anything about this part of Boston, from her drive in she did know that the T stopped to pick up passengers on the street to her right. Maybe he'd walked that way.

I'll go to the T stop and no further, she told herself. This was above-and-beyond Good Samaritan behavior. She headed in that direction, scanning the crowd.

The guy is long gone. He has to be.

But imagining what Bea would say if she turned around and went back into the restaurant kept her going.

She stopped at the big intersection with the T stop— Beacon Street, according to the sign. She stepped to the side, out of the stream of pedestrians crossing the street, and looked.

The clock tower building with the pharmacy inside was on the far diagonal corner of the intersection. A taqueria on another corner. A fancy bank that advertised a coffee bar on the third. Behind her, further down Beacon, she saw a Trader Joe's.

A fool's errand, she thought. She counted to twenty, giving her search the old college try. A green train wheezed its way up Beacon towards the waiting crowd at the T stop.

Guess it's time for pad thai, she thought. A twinge of guilt struck her, and she glanced around one more time.

And that's when she spotted him.

The man with the salt-and-pepper hair, wearing the dark jacket, hustled across the street. Now juggling a Trader Joe's bag along with his papers, he was clearly trying to make the train, which had stopped for passengers.

"Hey!" Andrea called. "Hey!"

It was hopeless. He wouldn't know she was hey-ing him!

She went to the edge of the sidewalk, just as the light allowing oncoming traffic turned green. Cars whizzed down Beacon and she jumped back.

"Sir!" she yelled again, waving her arms.

The man, unsurprisingly, didn't even glance in her direction. He disappeared around the front of the train, and by the time the traffic slowed and the light changed, he was already sardined into the green car. She raced across the street to the median, where the train stop was, anyway, even though she knew it was useless.

And as the train pulled away, Andrea's heart sank.

What am I going to tell Bea?

It was almost as though *their* tickets were the ones that had gone MIA.

As Andrea trudged back to the restaurant, she tried to shake off the disappointment. She and Bea were still going to the concert. Missing Ticket Lady had a (somewhat improbable) plan to get in. Pad thai awaited her.

By the time she pulled open the door, she'd almost brought herself out of her funk. Spotting her niece's hopeful expression brought it back.

"No luck," she said, sliding into her seat. "I'm sorry."

Bea looked crestfallen. "It's okay, Auntie. You tried."

"I guess," Andrea said. She glanced at the table. "Did you order yet?"

Bea nodded. "I got you the pad thai, but they left a menu so you could look at drinks or if you wanted anything else —especially since I ate all the spring rolls."

Andrea laughed and picked up her menu. Her stomach growled again as she opened it. Papers slid out onto her lap.

Andrea glanced down, expecting to see a specials menu. And she did see one—but there was a second piece of paper. *Cocktails!* she thought.

But why was there a barcode on the cocktails menu? And why did it read—

"Styrofoam Rockets!" she blurted. "Holy moly!"

"What?" Bea leaned over.

Andrea jumped up from her seat. The girls with the lost ticket had opened the door and were about to leave the restaurant.

"I've got it!" she yelled, waving the piece of paper over her head. "Hey! Stop!"

The girls spun to face her. "What?"

Andrea crossed the restaurant in four big leaps.

"I've got it," she said, unsure if the buzz she felt was from excitement or low blood sugar. "It was inside the menu." She thrust the printout at Quinny, whose puzzled expression turned to one of absolute joy as she realized what was on the paper.

She squealed and threw her arms around Andrea. "Thank you so much! Oh my gosh, I can't believe you found it!" Her friends also cheered and hugged Andrea. "You're amazing."

Andrea smiled and stood while they made a fuss and told the hostess that they'd like to buy Andrea a well-deserved drink. When they finally left the restaurant with a promise to hang on to the ticket for dear life, Andrea sank back into her seat at the table.

"Good job, Auntie." Bea grinned and Andrea smiled back.

The waitress brought over not only their food, but a few other appetizers. "On the house," the waitress said as she placed the plates on the table. "You were so nice to those girls."

Andrea smiled and thanked the woman, then dove into her pad thai like a ravenous beast.

"Just think, Auntie," Bea said, "we haven't even gotten to the concert yet. I wonder what else is going to happen?"

"Hopefully nothing," Andrea said between bites. "Hopefully not a thing."

Don't Forget Your Lederhosen

G. J. Crespo

PAULO PEEKED into the lobby of the Vietnamese restaurant. Colton was never on time, but he had to check. Some kid that had to be old enough to know better tapped on a fish tank while his parents scanned their phones. *In or out, people, don't block the entrance.* He backed out and scanned the street. No Colton. *Dude's always late.*

No sense hanging with the clueless family, so Paulo walked past a yoga place and found a brick wall to lean against. He closed his eyes for a few seconds and settled into waiting mode. *Plenty of time before the game.* He rolled his neck and paid attention to the people passing by. Couples, groups, single people, different colors and shapes, but all interesting in their own ways. He remembered a game he used to play with his sister and started making up stories about anyone that looked interesting.

Five people with papers and notebooks waiting in front of the restaurant. *Study group? Too old. Book group? No books. What's with all the papers? Writers? Poets? Maybe they were on their way to a poetry slam for epic-writing poets.* Another person joined them, and they went in. He turned his attention back to the people walking by. *Yankees fan with a Sox fan. Obviously married. Might as well be a Republican and a Democrat. After years of counseling, they can finally forgive each other for having the absolute worst taste in sports teams. Almost.*

Paulo checked his phone. No messages from Colton. *Five minutes before he was on time and twenty minutes before he'll actually show his ass up.* Colton had sold him a ticket for tonight's game against the Yankees. Paulo could not believe how expensive it was, but he hadn't been to a game since last fall, and this promised to be a good one. Two players, one from each team, were one hit away from franchise records and Colton's family's season tickets were in prime home run territory. If he could somehow be the one that caught a ball, he could sell it for a small fortune; much more than the price of the ticket and even worth putting up with Colton's brother, Corbin's high-fives and "bros" for nine innings.

A girl walked up to the front of the restaurant and peered into the lobby. She checked her phone and frowned, then stepped back from the doorway. *What's her story?* When he looked closer, she seemed familiar, but Paulo wasn't sure where he'd seen her before. *Somebody's Instagram?* She glanced at Paulo and then turned away and leaned against a parking meter. Her blue glasses triggered his memory. Colton had said he was meeting someone. *Some new girl he met somewhere. What was her name?*

He pulled his phone out and did a quick check. There was a picture of the two of them at a bar. Colton had tagged her as Natalie, no last name. Paulo was tired of leaning against the wall and Natalie looked semi-bored. *Might as well talk to a cute girl while I wait.* He walked over and caught her attention. "Are you waiting for Colton?"

She cocked an eyebrow at him. "Maybe."

What's with the look? I'm not asking her for spare change. "Maybe as in you don't know if you're waiting for him or *maybe* as in I should walk away and not bother you?"

She gave him a half-smile. "Maybe as in, I'm waiting for him and he's late."

Paulo laughed. "I'm waiting for him, too. I'm Paulo, his roommate from college. For the record, he's never on time."

"I've been noticing that." She gave him a full smile this time. *Nice dimples.* "I'm Natalie. He didn't say anybody was joining us for dinner."

"I'm not. I owe him money for a Sox ticket." Paulo pointed to his t-shirt.

Natalie nodded. "We're going to see a band tonight, but I have a sneaking suspicion he'd rather be going to the game." She seemed to want to say more, but she stopped herself.

Paulo nodded. "Well, the band must be pretty good because it's hard to pass up the opportunity to scream 'Yankees suck!' for three hours straight." She had deep brown eyes and her dark, curly hair showed red and orange highlights from the sun. He looked down at his shoes so he wouldn't keep staring at her.

Natalie said, "God, that's become like the state motto. I was at a Celtics game in the middle of winter and the crowd started chanting. And they were playing the Lakers. What's with that?"

Paulo looked up. How did Colton always get pretty girls to go out with him? He wasn't all that good looking, and he usually talked more than he listened, but somehow they were attracted to him. "Yeah, it's not really my thing, but Colton and his brothers get into it. What band are you going to see? Would I know them?"

"Probably not. They're opening for another band and unless you grew up in western Mass, I doubt you've ever heard of them."

"I don't know, maybe I have. Try me."

She tucked her hair behind her ear and rolled her eyes. "If you have, I'll be shocked; Betty Bleu with an 'eu' like in French."

Paulo squinted at her, searching his brain for a witty come-back. "Betty with an 'eu.' Right. Aren't they an all-girl, hip-hop, honky-tonk, death metal, fusion band that only does Patsy Cline covers in *Lord of the Rings* hobbit costumes?"

Natalie snorted out a laugh and shook her head. "Not even close. Try a folk-rock trio with two guys and a girl." Paulo liked that she wasn't embarrassed by the snort.

"That was my second guess." He blushed when she grinned at him. "You're right, I've never heard of them."

"I told you." She looked at her phone and sighed.

"What time is the show?"

"They come on at eight, but I wanted to talk to the singer before the show. She and I went to school together. We were besties until she joined the band. Now I hardly ever see her."

Paulo checked his phone. *Ten minutes late.* Natalie said, "What time is the game?"

"Eight. They usually start at seven, but it's the Yankees, so ESPN is covering it and if I was home, I'd have to listen to them go on about how wonderful New York is." He stopped when she raised an eyebrow at him. "You're not a fan, are you?"

"Not really. Celtics and Pats, but not baseball or hockey." She shifted her feet and leaned back against the parking meter. "So, you and Colton were roommates?"

Paulo shrugged. "Yeah, he was in my suite. We don't hang out much or anything. His family has season tickets and when he posted that he had one for sale, I jumped. I lucked out and was the first to contact him."

Natalie nodded and didn't seem to have anything to add, but he didn't want the conversation to die. "How did you meet Colton?"

She raised her eyebrows and took a breath. "His cousin married my cousin, and we were both in the wedding party." She paused for a second before she continued. "He was funny and a good dancer, so when he asked me out, I figured, why not?" She paused again. "Our first date was kind of a disaster, so the concert is supposed to be a do-over."

Paulo looked down the street and saw Colton strutting his way towards them. *Just like the bantam roosters on Tia Edna's farm; small, but louder than every other bird in the yard.* Paulo pointed his chin down the street. "Fifteen minutes late.

Right on time." Natalie gave him a puzzled look, but Paulo shook his head. "Never mind, just being a wise-ass."

Colton greeted Paulo with a handshake and a slap on the shoulder. "P-man, long time, no see. You psyched for the game?" He turned to Natalie for a hug, and Paulo turned away and tried not to listen to their hushed conversation. He heard Colton mutter, "We have plenty of time. Don't worry."

Paulo reached into his pocket for a wad of bills and waved it at Colton. "Exact amount."

"Thanks. The stupid app sends you a tax form if you go over their limit. It totally sucks." He did a quick count and said, "You got the link, right? Just show it at the gate and don't forget they don't take cash at the concessions anymore."

Paulo nodded to Natalie. "Nice to meet you," and turned to leave.

Colton put his hand out. "What's your hurry? You should have dinner with us so we can catch up. Natalie won't mind, right?" They both looked to her, and she shrugged her shoulders. Colton said, "See, I told you." He turned and opened the door for the both of them. "You'll never guess who I ran into last week. Remember Benzie? You should see him. He's gone all Wall Street. He's working a million hours a week but raking in the bucks. I'm totally jealous."

Paulo turned to Natalie. "I can just grab some food at Fenway. I don't want to interrupt."

She looked at him and then at Colton, who had gone ahead and let the door close behind him. She sighed and said, "No, it's fine. You guys can catch up." Paulo could tell she wasn't a hundred percent enthused, so he started to make an excuse to leave, but she held her hand up. "No, really. It's fine. I'm dying to hear all about *Benzie*, too."

Paulo laughed and held the door open for her. "I'm sure it will be almost as exciting as listening to me talk about baseball." That got him a little snort and a shake of her head.

The hostess led them to a table near the window, and Colton took his phone out and sat down. Paulo let Natalie choose the seat across from Colton before he sat down next to him. The waitress took their drink orders, and before they could settle into a conversation, Colton's phone chimed with text messages. Instead of muting the phone, he leaned back in his chair and tapped out a response.

Paulo caught Natalie giving Colton a little stink-eye and saw why their first date might have been a disaster. She glanced his way. *Well, if he's going to ignore her.* "So, when was the last time you saw your friend's band play?"

"It's been over a year. They spent some time on the west coast, playing clubs and bars but not getting noticed much. They were about to give up and come home when they connected with the drummer for the Styrofoam Rockets at one of their gigs. Turns out he had been following them on Instagram and drove an hour to catch one of their shows in Portland. Next thing they know, they're opening up for the Rockets while they do a couple of warm-up shows in Boston and New York before they go on tour in Europe."

Paulo nodded his head. "That's pretty amazing. You didn't say they were opening for the Rockets. I thought that show was sold out. How'd you even get tickets?"

She grinned. "Guest list. It pays to know the warm-up band."

"That's pretty cool. Too bad your friend can't go to Europe as well. My sister did a semester abroad in Madrid and she got to visit at least a dozen cities while she was there."

Natalie nodded. "I did the same thing junior year; except I was in Rome." She glanced at Colton, who was still laughing and texting away on his phone.

Paulo nudged him with his elbow. "Hey, we should order if you guys want to make the show on time."

Colton stopped texting and said, "Sure. Whatever. I'm going to hit the can first." He left his phone on the table and got up to find the bathroom. His phone chimed again, and Natalie read the name on the screen upside down. She frowned and said, "Who's Justine? That name sounds familiar." Paulo winced. He didn't want to rat Colton out, but he was being a dick by ignoring Natalie and texting with his old girlfriend. Natalie's expression went flat, and she picked up her phone. "Never mind, I can just check his Instagram." Paulo wanted to say something while she tapped and scrolled, but their drinks arrived and he busied himself with his beer.

Natalie muttered, "Fabulous," then placed her phone face down and turned to stare out the window. Paulo tried to think of something to say, but he had nothing. *How can he be so clueless?* Natalie took a breath and turned to face him. "Look, this isn't working out. I think I'm just going to head out."

Even though Colton deserved to be dumped, Paulo didn't want Natalie to leave. "Seriously? I can talk to him if you want me to."

She shook her head. "I don't think Colton will even notice. This happened the last time. He spent half the night on his phone, except texting with his old girlfriend makes it a hundred times worse."

"What about the concert? You can't go alone."

He saw a flash of anger in her eyes. "I don't need an escort. I'm perfectly capable of going to a club by myself."

Paulo blushed, embarrassed that she took him the wrong way. "I didn't mean it like that. It's just more fun when you go with someone." He took a breath. "But you're right. It sucks being ignored, so I guess I don't blame you if you want to leave."

The anger faded from her eyes. "Sorry for snapping. I don't like being underestimated."

"That wasn't my intent."

Colton came back, laughing loudly. "Whoa, you guys missed it. Someone on the other side was choking and this waiter dude gave them a Heinrich and they hurled this wad of shrimp across the room. It was epic."

Natalie gave him a flat stare. "It's *Heimlich*."

Colton sat down. "No way. Heimlich is like some Nazi dude from World War Two. Heimlich Zimmerman or something like that."

Natalie shook her head as if to clear it. "So, how's Justine? You guys were having quite the chat before you got up."

Paulo leaned away as Colton's face fell. "She's good. She was just asking about something." His pause was way too long. "She's just an old friend."

Natalie rolled her eyes. "Please, I'm not stupid." She held her phone up and showed Colton a picture of him and Justine drunk at the beach. He was wrapped around her and kissing her neck while she took the photo.

Paulo picked up a menu and pretended to study it. *The Lemongrass Chicken sounds decent.*

Colton stammered. "Whatever, that was taken like three months ago. We broke up." His phone chimed again and Justine's name lit up the screen.

Natalie held her hand out. "Then you won't mind if I read what you guys have been texting about."

Paulo shifted his menu so he could see Colton's reaction. "That's like an invasion of my privacy. I wouldn't ask to read text messages from your old boyfriends."

"I wouldn't text my old boyfriends when I'm on a date."

"But you still text them, right?"

She glared at him. "No, I don't text any of my old boyfriends, and I don't spend all my time on my phone when I'm out with someone." She dropped her phone in her purse and pushed her chair back. "I need to use the bathroom."

Colton let out his breath and said, "Go to the hostess desk and turn right. It's down the hall."

Natalie eyeballed him over her glasses and said, "I think I can find the bathroom on my own." She shouldered her bag and walked towards the entrance. Colton picked up his phone and checked his messages as soon as she rounded the corner.

Paulo punched Colton on the arm. "What the hell's your problem? You're being a total dick."

"Don't you start in on me. You're supposed to back me up."

"Why would I back you up? You've been glued to that phone since we sat down. What's Justine have to say that's so important?"

Colton took a breath and let it out. "She wants to get back together. She invited me down to Falmouth for the weekend."

Colton's screen lit up again, and he was too busy texting to see Natalie come back from the bathroom and stop short when she saw him tapping away on his phone. She caught Paulo's eye, shook her head, and walked out of the restaurant. Paulo leaned to his left and saw her turn right towards Coolidge Corner.

Paulo smacked Colton on the shoulder again. Colton stared at him blankly. "What?"

"Natalie just walked out, and you were too busy texting Justine to even notice."

Colton rolled his eyes. "You're shitting me. I gave up a Sox game because she wanted to see her friend's band."

Paulo said, "So you're just going to let her go?"

He looked down at his phone screen and shrugged his shoulders. "I mean, I like Natalie, but Justine says she'll give me another chance."

Paulo said, "Give me my money back. You can have the Sox ticket." He looked out the window, but Natalie was nowhere in sight.

"Why? What are you going to do?"

"I'm going to see about a concert."

"No way. You think she's going to choose you over me? She's totally out of your league."

"She already chose nobody over you, so I figure my chances are pretty good." He pulled out his phone. "Just give me the money and I'll send the ticket back to you."

Colton shook his head and handed over the cash. "Whatever. You owe me for your beer and her drink."

Paulo tossed a twenty at Colton and scooted his chair back. "Have fun at the game," and rushed out the door.

Paulo ran as fast as he could down to Coolidge Corner, dodging a turning car in front of the bagel shop and running across Beacon Street against the light. The platform for the inbound train was empty and a trolley rumbled about a quarter mile down the tracks. There was no way he could catch up with it. *Awesome. I probably just missed her*. He looked for the next trolley and saw nothing but empty track. *Perfect. Just perfect.*

Natalie stepped out of Trader Joe's and slipped the chocolate bar into her purse. She had no regrets about walking out on Colton, but she still needed to eat. She wasn't familiar with Coolidge Corner, so she scanned the shops across the street for a place to grab a quick bite. *Burritos, no. Dunkin', no thanks. Why did that bagel place have to be closed?* Her eyes came to a stop at the trolley platform. That Paulo guy was standing there. *Seriously? What does he want?*

She checked her phone. *Still plenty of time.* She could wait him out. She wasn't going back even if Colton came crawling on his knees, so she sure as hell wasn't going to be fetched by his errand boy. *Why did I agree to a second date with someone surgically attached to their phone? Never again. Learn from your mistakes, girl.* She leaned against a light pole and watched Paulo pace up and down the platform. Instead of heading back to the restaurant, he kept looking down the tracks for the next train. *Huh. Maybe he's not looking for me. Maybe he left Colton all to his sorry-ass self.*

She waited another minute, then crossed the street, keeping a tall guy between her and Paulo until she could slip behind him. He didn't even notice her, so she took a minute to check him out. *If he's not trying to drag me back to Colton, I guess I could talk to him. Maybe he knows someplace I can eat before the show.*

Natalie gave Paulo a hard poke between the shoulder blades. "What are you doing here?" He turned around and she gave him her *don't even try to bullshit me* look. "I'm not going back, so don't waste your time."

Paulo laughed out loud. "Why would you? Colton was being a total ass. I'm surprised you lasted as long as you did."

"Then why are you here? You could have had dinner with Colton and still made it to the game."

He took a breath and said, "I'm not going to the game. I sold the ticket back to Colton."

"Wait, I thought you were going to catch some home run ball and sell it for a million dollars."

He shrugged his shoulders and looked down at the ground between them. "They don't like it when you keep the ball. They offer to trade it for tickets or autographed stuff. With my luck, I'd catch the Yankees ball and end up with a bunch of crap from my least favorite team."

She laughed. "You could sell it, though. Somebody out there would probably pay big bucks for autographed Yankees crap."

"Yeah, but I guess that's Colton's problem now."

She shook her head. "I doubt it. He wouldn't see the ball coming because he'd be on his damn phone texting his old girlfriend." *Dammit, why did I say that? Just move on already.*

Natalie watched Paolo scuff the platform with the toe of his shoe. It took him a few seconds before he looked up at her. "Can we not talk about Colton? I mean, we can if you need to vent or something, but the truth is I sold the ticket because I wanted to talk to you."

Didn't see that coming. "I'm here, so talk."

He took a deep breath. "I know you don't need an escort or anything, but if it's cool, I'd like to go see the concert with you."

And I definitely wasn't expecting that. "You want to see some band you never even heard of?"

He shrugged. "I don't know. Maybe I'm really into emo, bluegrass, skin-head, hybrid music performed by people in lederhosen and cowboy boots."

She couldn't hold back a smile. "Wait, I thought it was hobbit costumes."

He shrugged again. "I hear they like to mix it up." His face blushed red. "So, I know you barely know me, but I was hoping you wouldn't mind if I tagged along."

Seriously? She frowned and squinted her eyes at him. *Not my usual type, but not like that's been working.* "I don't know. You're right, I hardly know you. You could be hiding some serious character flaws." She tried not to smile when he rolled his eyes. "How long can you go without checking your phone?"

"Hours." He pulled his phone out and held it up. "And I even deleted my last girlfriend from my contacts when we broke up."

Yeah, right. "Show me. What's her name?"

He opened his contacts and handed her his phone. "Jennifer Lopez. She'd be under J.Lo." She stared at him over her glasses. *I may be from western Mass, but I'm not an idiot.* He crossed his heart. "I'm serious. That was her name. Jennifer Claudia Lopez Colon. The J.Lo was a joke."

She scrolled through the contacts, noting that most of them were guys, and handed the phone back to him. "Okay, I suppose you can come, but only if you promise to keep that thing in your pocket." *Oh my God, tell me I didn't just say that.* He nodded, and she smiled at him. "And don't forget your lederhosen. You can't get in the door without them."

Triple Date

A SHORT GHOST STORY

Megan M. Mullin

I NEVER THOUGHT there would be anything worse than working a busy lunch at The Three Taps, but that was before I was also being haunted by the literal ghost of my ex.

"Kate! Can I talk to you for a second?" Zac's flickering outline appeared beside me, bobbing impatiently from side to side, as I attempted to smile while handing menus to a table full of chatty moms in yoga gear. A silvery puff of air escaped my lips as I said, "I'll be right back to take your order!" The air around Zac—and now, consequently, me —was always so cold. I prayed my wintry breath was hidden by the early afternoon light pouring through the pub's windows.

I speed-walked to the waitress station and pretended to straighten the bread baskets. "Zac," I hissed, knowing he'd followed me as goosebumps raised on my bare arms. "You need to stop trying to talk to me WHILE I AM WORK-ING. People are going to think I'm crazy." Zac—despite the fact he was an intangible being—leaned casually against the wall of the small, closet-like space. "No more so than usual," he grinned. I glared back. How dare he manage to still be so goddamn handsome, even in death?

"Hilarious," I muttered. "Look, I can only hide back here for so long. What is it?" I glanced over my shoulder to see if anyone was walking by, and accidentally looked straight through Zac's torso in the process. I shuddered. Zac had been haunting me—and only me—at The Three Taps since he was hit by a city bus about a month ago, but apparently you never get used to your ex-boyfriend being translucent.

Happy for my attention, he stood up straight and began bouncing on the balls of his non-existent feet. "So, I was hanging out behind the bar just now, and I heard this guy saying he is going to see The Styrofoam Rockets at The House of Blues. TONIGHT." I couldn't help but smile to see this signature Excited Zac move. In life, every emotion Zac possessed had a physical counterpart: when stressed, he messed up his hair. Bored or anxious was accompanied by table drumming. And excited partnered with bouncing. The fact these uniquely human, very physical quirks had followed him after death still caught me off-guard. It would be very easy to believe Zac was still very much alive and well if not for the fact no one else could see or hear him but me.

"Um, that's cool? I didn't know they were touring." Styrofoam Rockets was Zac's all-time favorite band. I liked them too, but his devotion was border-line obsession. He'd seen them every time they'd come through Boston and had even traveled out of state for shows. Once, he'd been on vacation in Italy and literally extended his stay a day because Styrofoam Rockets were playing at some little bar in Milan the day he was supposed to have been flying out of Rome. He was a man possessed.

Well, a ghost possessed now, I guess. Except… Zac couldn't see them this time. He couldn't leave The Three Taps. Every attempt he'd made to exit the building, he'd find himself right back behind the bar he used to work.

"Neither did I! I had been so wrapped up in Olivia's wedding planning, I must have missed the announcement." He made a funny face at this admission—oh, did I mention Zac had been engaged to someone else before he died? Yeah. Anyway, guilt and something else—a flicker of resentment?—flashed across Zac's face, but true to form, he pulled himself back together in an instant. "I really need to see them, Kate. You know Frank will never play them in here." Zac was not wrong about that. Frank, owner of The Three Taps, was very particular about the music played in the pub. Soft, inoffensive, and easily chatted over. The Styrofoam Rockets were the polar opposite of that.

"But… you can't, Zac. How would you get there?" The shifty expression that now took hold of Zac's features made it abundantly clear he had already had a plan.

"Absolutely not," I whispered as I stalked back to the table of SAHMs. Zac kept pace with me, floating across the floor—a new ghostly trick he'd recently learned. "Come on, Katie. It'll just be a MILD possession. Just for tonight!" I narrowed my eyes at him for a split second before plastering on my fake waitress smile and taking the table's order. Then I spun on my heel and practically ran back to the kitchen. Unbelievable. While we were dating, Zac, more often than not, made the decisions of where to eat, what movie to see, what wine to order. At the time, I shrugged and went along with whatever he wanted to do since I was just happy to be along for the ride. After he dumped me, however, I realized how infrequently I had taken the wheel during that ride. And now here he was again, asking me not just to give up my evening but my literal body to go see a show.

"Kate. Please. This might be the last time I ever hear their music. It's not like I had a lot of warning before I shuffled off my mortal coil." His big, formerly brown eyes stared at the floor. "If it doesn't work, or if it's painful or too scary, we don't have to go through with it."

I sighed. "Let me think about it," I said and pushed through the swinging kitchen doors. Zac didn't follow.

I wordlessly handed the order to Berto, one of our line cooks. "You awake, Kate? Hungover again, maybe?" he teased, turning back to the flattop range currently sizzling with three thick burgers.

I wish, I thought. Hungover would definitely be preferable today. Seeing nothing ready to go out yet, I headed for the doors. Then I heard my name being called.

It was Jamie, our tall, ginger-haired head chef. Unlike his predecessor Eddie—a short-tempered New Yorker who found the kitchen culture in Boston (or at least, The Three Taps) far too laid-back for his taste—Jamie was quiet and methodical. You might have gotten your food faster out of Eddie's kitchen, but it wouldn't have tasted as good as Jamie's. "Hey, Kate," he said, his hands still deftly moving from one pan to the other. "You still free tonight?"

Shit.

Last night, Jamie had asked if I wanted to check out this Vietnamese place for dinner after our shifts ended today. Jamie had never asked if I wanted to do anything with him outside of work before, but in the wake of Zac's death lots of people had become super solicitous. Checking in on me, bringing me snacks, asking if I wanted to talk over coffee. It was still a surprise, but I found myself saying sure.

"Ummm, yeah! Tonight! Yeah, totally." I flashed him a thin smile and hustled back out into the dining room. There it was. I had a built-in excuse to say no to Zac's crazy idea. *Shoot, sorry, I forgot I had plans. Maybe you can possess me some other time.* It was the perfect out.

But as usual, when it came to all things Zac-related, I was already caving. The poor guy died. He was stuck here 24/7. He doesn't know how he got here or why. The least I could do was let him see his favorite band one last time. Even if it involved a little "mild possession."

We'd just have to swing by a restaurant first.

A few hours later, my shift was over. I still hadn't given Zac a definitive answer and he—to his credit—had left me alone for the rest of the afternoon. I stood dithering in the waitress station, fighting with a knot in my apron.

"Hey, want me to get that?"

Jamie's orange-red head popped into frame. I jumped—usually it was an actual ghost appearing out of nowhere to startle me; now I had to worry about chefs too? I shrugged, then nodded; undoing knots was not my forté. Three swift tugs and I was free. "Thanks," I said as I crumpled the short black apron into a ball. Jamie gave a half smile and hesitated.

"Well. I'm going to head home and shower first if that's ok. Want to meet me at the restaurant in an hour? I'll text you the address." His voice was even softer than usual, and he awkwardly shoved his hands into his pockets. I nodded, tried to smile, then side-stepped out of the cubby with a hasty wave.

I hustled towards the back exit of the pub, looking around for Zac's foggy aura. Sure enough, there he was, fidgeting in the corner. "Hey! Hi. Um. Did you... did you think about..." I put up a hand to stop him.

"Let's give this a try before I change my mind," I said quietly, looking over my shoulder to make sure no one was there to witness what looked like me talking to myself. "Just make it quick." As if I was getting a flu shot or having my bikini line waxed.

Zac smiled from ear to ear. "Thanks, Katie. I swear, if it gets too intense we don't have to—"

"Let's just see if it even works."

Ghost Zac reached out, as if he was going to take my hands. I reached back, knowing full well I wouldn't be able to touch him. His outstretched fingers slid through mine like a cold fog. His eyes locked onto mine and he nodded once, like he was saying *brace yourself.* Then he leaned forward slowly and intentionally, as if he was going to pass through me.

I immediately felt as if I'd been doused in ice water. I gasped, stumbled back, and hit the wall. My eyes swam, a disembodied wind began blowing through my brain, and the ice water sensation continued to creep up and until I was submerged—

"Whoa, Katie, your eyesight! What the heck. Have you been to see an eye doctor?"

The voice was mine. The words were not. My hands waved in front of my face. *Zac! Is that you?*

My hands fell back to my sides. My body started pacing the small back room. Neither of these actions were my idea; I was just along for the ride. Then I heard Zac's voice, but it was emanating from inside my head. It sounded tinny, like it was trapped in an old-school metal lunchbox from the 80s. *I... I think we did it. Is this okay? How do you feel?*

I tried to raise my arms, but they stayed stubbornly down. I tried to stop walking, but the pacing continued. *Weird, Zac. I feel very weird. Like I'm paralyzed. Or .. no. Like I'm a Muppet. And you're Jim Henson with your hand up my butt.* He snort-laughed. *It's not funny, Zackary!*

Zac continued to giggle. *I'm sorry, I'm sorry. It's a little funny. Ok. Let me see if I can... turn over the controls, so to speak.* My body stopped pacing and stood very still. Zac closed my eyes and in the darkness I felt that whooshing wind settle into a gentle breeze. *Ok. How's this?* He said in my head. *Try opening your eyes.*

With effort, I raised my eyelids. I have never appreciated the ability to open my own damn eyes. I took a tentative step forward. I felt a little resistance, as if I was walking into a headwind, but I could do it. "All right," I whispered out loud to the Zac in my head. "Let's see what happens when I go outside."

I pushed open the heavy back door and slowly stepped into the late afternoon sunlight. The wind in my head picked up a bit, making me dizzy, and I stumbled into The Three Taps' recycling bins. I steadied myself on the pub's brick exterior. *Zac? Can you hear me? Are you still there?*

There was a breath of silence. Had I lost him? Panic rose from my guts.

It's okay. I'm okay! I'm still here. This is amazing. I almost forgot what this felt like. What SUN felt like! He sounded louder. Stronger. His infectious laugh echoed around in my mind. *Holy shit, Katie, we did it! But*—I felt the wind whooshing even faster now—*wait. You have a DATE tonight?*

"I do NOT. Wait. How the hell did you know that?" I whispered aloud as I started walking up Centre Street towards where I parked my car. *You're going out with Jamie the chef?* He continued. I unlocked my beat-up blue Beetle, tossed in my purse, and hopped inside. "NO. I mean, yes, but we're just checking out this restaurant he's heard good things about. It's not a date. Now how. Did. You. Know. That?!"

Zac didn't immediately answer. And in the quiet I heard— barely a whisper—*Ugh how do I explain this?*

"How do you explain WHAT?"

Christ! Can… can you hear me thinking too, Katie?

Oh, sweet mother of God. Not only was I possessed by the ghost of my ex-boyfriend, apparently we could also now hear each other's thoughts. I was living my nightmares.

"Look. I don't have the capacity to figure out all of… whatever is happening right now, Zac," I said. "So just for now, do me a favor. Stay PERFECTLY STILL so I can drive home. You never learned to drive stick."

Zac and I bolted up the stairs to my apartment. I say Zac and I because it was very much a non-coordinated group effort. In our shared panic, we kept switching places—one minute I was steering the ship, the next I felt like a very confused passenger. Finally, we crashed my poor addled body through the door and into the worn leather armchair in my living room.

"Ok, I gotta call Jamie and tell him I can't come. This is way weirder than I expected." I pulled my phone out of my purse; I saw a text from Jaime—probably that address he promised.

What? No! Oh my God, no you HAVE to go. When was the last time you went out on a date?

I willed myself to not even think about the answer to that question.

"First of all, it's not a date. Second, even if it was, I am not in the greatest shape to casually hang out with another human being right now. He'll think I've had a stroke."

Zac laughed at that. Then I heard him sigh. *Look, even if you don't think it's a date, you should still go. I just... I'm...* The internal wind dropped to barely a breeze. My face suddenly flushed, though I wasn't personally feeling awkward or embarrassed. No more so than usual, anyway. Was Zac blushing?

I mean, we're going out to the show anyway, right? Might as well practice this whole possession thing before we get there.

Oh right. The show. I should probably see if they still have tickets.

Five minutes later, I had secured General Admission for one. I guess getting last-minute tickets is easier when you're alone. Well. Sort of alone. This whole possession thing would never be normal. But it was nice to be able to talk to Zac outside of work. As soon as I thought that, however, I instantly regretted it. Because sure enough...

It's nice to hang out with you too, Katie. Now let's get you changed for your not-date.

Changed?!

"Sir. May I remind you we are no longer dating. You are not privy to what's under this very stylish polo shirt."

I felt myself flush again, but this was a furious blush—as if we were both turning red simultaneously. *I'll... close my eyes?*

"You CAN'T, dummy, they are MY EYES."

Yeah, but you can't go out in this. Zac took charge and gestured to my Three Taps uniform: Black collared short-sleeved shirt, black pants, grease-stained sneakers. All of which also held the scent of a hundred lunch orders. He had a point. *You should probably shower too—*

"I'm going to stop you right there. I have dry shampoo and I can wash my face. And throw on some perfume. I am definitely drawing the line at co-showering." I felt the heat of another double-blush.

Yup! Yup, yup, yup. Solid point.

I grabbed a clean shirt and a pair of jeans and tossed them onto my bed. Then I stood paralyzed. This was stupid. Zac and I dated for years; it was nothing he hadn't seen before. But still…

What if … what if we blindfolded ourselves? Zac suggested.

"WHAT."

No seriously! You're doing me a huge favor; the last thing I want to do is make you uncomfortable. Let's grab one of those cute neck scarves you never wear and… I mean, it's not like you've never dressed in the dark before, right?

I couldn't help it. I busted out into an uncontrollable fit of giggles. "This feels like some kind of supernatural trust exercise," I said, but I started fishing around in my top drawer for one of those aforementioned cute scarves my mom always gave me that I never could figure out how to wear.

Getting dressed blindfolded, while your body is supernaturally compromised, is just as awkward as you'd imagine. We put my head through my shirt's armhole and tripped putting on the jeans, but all in all I guess it could have been worse. After freshening up the rest of me as best we could, it was time to head out on the world's strangest triple date.

I found parking around the corner from the Vietnamese place. Finding a spot in Brookline was almost as hard as finding street parking in Jamaica Plain, so I thanked the Parking Gods for this one stroke of good luck. *We have to hustle*, I thought to both of us; *I'll be late in a minute.*

Don't you mean WE'LL be late?

Another downside to Zac's ghost being in my head instead of floating in front of me, is that I couldn't glare at him.

We finally pushed open the glass door of the restaurant. The first thing I saw was a huge tank full of giant lethargic goldfish. *Probably koi,* Zac corrected. Resisting the urge to roll my eyes, I looked through the tank. Standing right on the other side was Jamie, waiting by the hostess stand, hands in pockets. He looked nice; he was wearing a green Henley top with the sleeves pushed part of the way up, exposing a slew of tattoos (an accessory most chefs seemed to have in common) and his hair looked clean and intentionally mussed instead of "I've been working in front of a stove all day" mussed.

See? I told you it was a date. Zac's disembodied voice should have sounded "told you so," but it almost sounded put-out. Pouty. I tried not to think about it, but of course:

No I don't! I bet it's just your nerves rubbing off on me. Now let's go in—stop staring at these fish, we look nuts. But I felt rooted to the spot. Because I was. Suddenly, Zac had the wheel again.

"Oh shit," I heard myself whisper.

Have you ever had one of those dreams where you know you're you, but it's almost like you're just watching the proceedings like a movie through your eyes? Now imagine it's real and your ex-boyfriend's ghost is walking your body up to someone you may or may not be on a date with.

"Hi there! Hi! Here I am!" Zac said in my voice, way too loud and WAY too cheerily. *Have you ever met me?* I hissed inside my head. *Settle down!*

Jamie startled slightly but composed himself just as quickly. "So you are," he grinned. "Our table is ready; I was just waiting here for you so we could sit down together." *A gentleman too*, Zac thought. If I could have whacked myself without looking insane, I would have.

Zac. You have to give me control. You don't know Jamie as well as I do.

I'm TRYING. I can't. I don't know what the problem is....

Well, what happened the last time you possessed someone?

Ha, ha—

"Uh, Kate? You coming?" Jamie was a few steps in front of me—us—and had turned to glance over his shoulder.

"Yup! Sure thing. Sorry, was just looking at these fish. What do you think—they're koi, right? Don't you think they're koi?" Zac prattled on in my voice (which also sounded higher than usual, as if he was trying to sound like a woman) as he widened our steps to catch up. *What is with you and these freaking fish?* I thought.

Jamie pulled out a chair and tilted his head quizzically. "Uh, I don't know. I thought they were just overgrown goldfish." *SEE,* I thought triumphantly. Zac waited for Jamie to sit, but he continued to stand there, hand on the back of the empty chair. Great. He's already completely weirded out by me. Us.

Suddenly, Zac thought *OH!* and sat down so abruptly I thought we were going to fall sideways off of the chair. "Thanks!" Zac chirped, thinking in the next second: *Okay, that was a first for me.*

WHAT was?

He pulled out the seat for you, Kate. This is one thousand percent a date.

Oh God. Of course. **Of course** the first date I've had since Zac broke up with me, Zac was also there. No, not just there, IN CHARGE. And he was the one who realized I was on a date before I did.

I'm sorry! I am trying to give you control; you're just not taking it. He hissed in my head, sounding frustrated and a little hurt. Then, *I... sorry, I didn't know this was your first...* Zac trailed off.

So far unaware that his dinner companion was currently possessed by a dead bartender, Jamie had taken the seat across from me—us—and pulled a pair of glasses out of his shirt pocket. *Since when does Jamie wear glasses?* They looked... cute. Studious.

"I didn't know you wore glasses," Zac asked for me.

Jamie's pale cheeks flushed a little. "They're not real glasses. Just readers from CVS. I noticed recently it was harder to read menus in dim restaurant light. I'm hoping I don't start to need them all the time—I'll have to get contacts; glasses will get all fogged up and dirty in the kitchen."

Looks like JAMIE is taking care of HIS eyesight, Zac thought. I was about to feebly protest when the next thing I knew, my arm shot across the table. "Mind if I try them on for a second?" I heard myself ask.

What the hell are you DOING—

Looking perplexed, Jamie slid the frames off his face and placed them in my outstretched hand. Wasting no time,

Zac popped the plastic-framed readers onto my face and picked up the menu.

Whoa.

See? You can actually SEE now. You need glasses. Kate—

I hated that he was right, but the proof was there in black and white—black and white type to be exact—that was suddenly bigger and crisper and clearer.

"I had a feeling I needed glasses, just wanted to prove it to myself," Zac quipped cheerily. *I swear to God, Zackary, this concert better be the best goddamn concert I've ever seen*—I fumed in my head. Jamie was smiling pleasantly as he took the glasses back.

"Well, they looked nice on you. A little big maybe." Jamie grinned. I definitely flushed. Zac made us fidget in the seat. *This is SO AWKWARD, Kate, just take over already! Look, I'll stay perfectly still.*

I tried to scratch my nose. Nothing. I tried reaching out for the menu. My arms lay stiff at my sides. The wind inside of my head had quieted to a light breeze again. It wasn't Zac taking over. I just **couldn't take control.** I felt lost. Lost in my head. Lost in my own body. Even broken up, even after he freaking DIED, I still let Zac take the lead. And now I was stuck.

"Kate? You okay?" Jamie had started reading the menu again but was now peering over the top at what I imagined looked like me doing my very best statue impression. I wanted to answer. To scream, "No, not really, I'm figuratively AND literally possessed by my ex at the moment." Instead, I heard Zac answer softly for me.

"Yeah, uh, just wondering where the restroom was," I suddenly felt myself standing, eyes scanning the restaurant. Jamie's mouth turned down a bit, but cut his chin across the room and said, "It's just past the hostess stand." Zac smiled and nodded for me, and the next thing I knew, we were power walking past tables towards the ladies' room.

What the hell are you doing? You can't go in the LADIES room, Zac!

Oh my God, calm down, you guys have stalls. I won't see anything. Anyway, we just need a sec—

Zac hesitated slightly when we reached the door before swinging it open a little too quickly, making the girl standing at the sinks jump.

"Sorry!" He said quickly, and I felt myself flush. Typical. The girl was younger and pretty, with dark bouncy hair and a pair of chic glasses. The frames were extra-large and bright blue—I could never pull off something so cool. *Yes you could, shut up,* Zac said.

The girl tucked her hair behind her ears and sighed. She looked just as happy to be here as I did. "No worries. I'm just kind of escaping in here, anyway. Ever been on a date that is going completely and utterly WRONG?" I started to laugh just as Zac guffawed, creating a very strange barking laugh that echoed in the small, tiled bathroom.

"Ahhhhh," Zac cleared my throat, embarrassed enough for both of us. "Sorry again—it's just, yeah. I definitely know what you mean." The girl half smiled and gave her curls one last pat.

"Good to know I'm not alone. Okay, wish me luck," she said as she left the bathroom with a steely look in her eye.

Yowza. I would hate to be on the receiving end of THAT look, Zac thought.

Hey, maybe whoever it is deserves it.

Maybe they do. He paused. *Kate... Katie. Look, I'm sorry. I—I never realized... This whole being dead thing has left me a lot of time to think about how I lived and... I never meant to make you feel that way. Like you were never in control.*

I suddenly wished I could see Zac.

Hey. That was a two-way street. Sure, you could have paid more attention, but I let you make all the calls. I could have spoken up more, too. At some point, you gotta take charge of your own life, right? I felt my shoulders droop. *Sorry! Bad choice of words.*

No, you're right. So do it. Take charge.

I felt my hands grip the cold sides of the sink and my head raised to look at myself in the mirror. As I locked onto my eyes—my own eyes—I saw a faint silver light flicker out in the center of my pupils. Then I raised **my** hands, fluffed **my** hair, and straightened **my** top. I had the wheel. And I gripped it tight.

Back at the table, a plate of summer rolls had appeared while I was finding myself in the restroom. Jamie looked up at me cautiously. "Everything ok?"

I sat down; I draped my napkin across my lap. I smiled across the table. "Totally fine. Hey, summer rolls, right? I love these." I heard Zac very faintly in the back of my head, *You do?*

Jamie passed me the plate. "Yeah, I remember you mentioning that once, so I figured I'd order us some before our mains." I snatched one of the veggie-shrimp- and pork-stuffed translucent wraps and took a grateful bite. "Good call," I said.

I felt Zac's presence drift further into the back of my head. Barely a breeze whispered around my thoughts. *Enjoy your date, Katie. I'll talk to you later at the concert.*

Jamie was musing aloud about which variation of phở noodle soup to order. I watched him with a small, reserved smile on my face—one hand lightly hanging on to Zac's disembodied self in my head, one hand firmly on the wheel.

Slacking Off

Wendy M. McDonald

IT'S NOT until my flight lands in Boston Friday afternoon, and we're allowed to use our phones again, that I get Tod's Slack messages.

> TOD: Tracey would you please send an email with the agenda for next week's meeting. I need to have the most recent version. The date of your event is rapidly approaching.

> TOD: Oh. I just saw your vacation status. Just answer when you get a minute and I will be out of your hair for a bit.

Ugh. Tod is the new event coordinator at the Old Potomac Conference Center in DC, where my employer holds our annual conference. I'm regretting giving Tod access to our conference-planning Slack channel because he's forever bugging us with minutiae and resend requests. Either he used to work for a micromanager, or he's never event-coordinated before, or he's outrageously disorganized, but I hope he mellows by the time our conference runs next month. Climate Action Now's conference is an annual meeting-of-minds with a dozen other East Coast climate activist organizations, and this is our first in-person conference since the pandemic shut everything down. We really want it to go well again.

I'm near the back of the plane and the doors just opened, so I message Tod back even though I'm sure I'll regret it.

> TRACEY: The email I sent this morning is the most recent version. I'll be back in the office Monday.

It's because of The Odious Tod that I worked a half-day today, instead of enjoying the whole morning by myself before heading to National for my three pm flight. I'm used to working long hours and weekends—I knew, when I signed on with CAN, that it's a tiny organization trying to make a big difference. But ever since Tod took over at Old Potomac, my workload has increased—especially the off-hours texts.

Damn, if I don't need this trip. I'm desperate to shake the stink of DC politics off my psyche, even if it's only for a weekend.

Still waiting for the throng ahead of me to trickle forward so I can step into the aisle, and ever the mom, I send Cal a text.

> MOM: We've landed. Make sure you thank the Robbinses again for letting you stay this weekend, and don't forget to give them the brownies I made. They're on the table.

> CAL: got it don't worry

> CAL: have fun mom

> CAL: but not too much fun, pbtbtbt

By the time I get through the security checkpoint and summon Heidi from the cell phone lot, it's just after five pm. She pulls her Honda Accord up to the curb, puts the flashers on, pops the trunk, and hops out.

Like me, Heidi is decked out in tight jeans and a Styrofoam Rockets tee from a few tours ago. She's painted her blonde hair in a pastel rainbow with some sort of hair wax, and arranged it into a pair of pigtails that somehow don't look remotely wrong on her, despite the fact that she's 51. But I'm not brave enough to attempt anything that might still be evident when I return to my real life Sunday afternoon, so my boring, mostly-still-brown hair is piled into a boring messy bun, and I've got a spare scrunchie on my wrist.

She pulls me in for a hug. "What's going on? You look stressed. You're supposed to be letting it all go for a few days."

"It's the job," I say, as another message comes in from Tod.

> TOD: Thanks. But even though you say you sent it this morning, I don't have it. Please resend.

I punch out a quick response designed to remind him that, even though it's after five on a Friday, there are plenty of people still in my office who aren't on vacation and who are perfectly capable.

> TRACEY: Steven and Addison were both copied on that email and can help you with a resend. I'm out of the office for the weekend. I will return on Monday.

I stuff the phone into my purse, where its buzzing will be less obvious if Tod sends anything else, and toss the ragged weekender bag I've had since college into Heidi's trunk before climbing into the passenger seat. A few minutes later, we're headed across a broad, curved overpass, then into a tunnel, Heidi cussing at drivers who can't hear her. Though I'm clearly in for a rough ride, it's actually reassuring to know her approach to other drivers hasn't changed since our years at Bowie State. I settle into my seat and try to pretend Tod won't be texting me several times more.

"I know I agreed to the hours and the pace when I accepted the position, but I'm tired of going in early and staying late. This year, since we had to pause conferences during the pandemic—and with the way climate change is happening faster than scientists calculated—the conference prep is all-consuming. I swear if Cal weren't such a freakishly responsible teenager, I don't know what I'd do."

She frowns. "I keep telling you to find a new job—a better one. You're topped out at CAN. In the meantime, you need an excellent bowl of phở, a night of musical abandon, and a walk on a proper New England beach."

"We've had this conversation before. First: I'm not moving to Boston; I'm a mid-Atlantic gal. Second: I like my nonprofit gigs. It makes me feel like I'm contributing something worthwhile to the world. Trying to save the planet, especially, matters to me."

The car ahead of us stops in the middle of the intersection. Heidi veers right, floors it, then screeches to a halt again behind a double-parked Ford minivan. "Tracey, when are you going to learn there's more than one way to make a contribution to the world and save the planet? And anyway, I'm not saying you should move to Boston...just that you should actually have a life outside your job."

"I don't know..." I say, feeling lame even as the words spill out. On the one hand, she's right, but on the other—do I even have the mental energy to find another way to save the planet besides working for CAN?

"Where's the concert, again?" That's why I've left Cal with his best friend's family this weekend: the Styrofoam Rockets show. They're huge in Canada, but down here almost nobody knows who they are, so they play little venues and don't even stop in all the big cities. This tour, they've skipped the DC area entirely, so when Heidi suggested I take a rare vacation and visit her so she could finally show Boston off to me, it was hard to say *No*.

Not that my sense of responsibility didn't stop me: *Cal's responsible, but he's only seventeen... the show's on a Thursday so I'd have to take time off work... flights are pretty pricey right now... Grey's been weird about his visitations recently...*

But Heidi had an answer for everything—all the way through covering my ticket with miles she had saved up, and pointing out that me taking my first round-trip flight since my honeymoon won't decimate the atmosphere—so here I am.

"House of Blues," she says, running a light so yellow it's practically red. "It's near Fenway."

I don't know what that means, but I nod and press my hand against the armrest along the side of the door to stave off my impulse to reach up for the *oh, shit* bar as the car lurches to a stop, cutting off a cabbie. "Cool," I say.

"It's more than cool," she says, "There's a little bar right next door—it's attached, actually—and—FUCK YOU, TOO, BUDDY!—and you can eat there before the show, or grab a beer after and hang with the band."

I snort. "Yeah, like the Styrofoam Rockets are going to go hang at the bar like some undiscovered band."

It's a relief to not have to be in the driver's seat for a change—either literally or figuratively—and I take the opportunity to zone out a little. Gazing out the window at the trees along the river, their leaves turning shades of amber and crimson, I can't help but think it would be beyond awesome to hit it off with—or hell, just *meet*—one of the guys from Styrofoam Rockets. I could use something fresh in my life. Cal thinks he has all the fun and most of the time he's right, but Grey and I used to be pretty wild when we were younger: dressing as Brad and Janet and reciting all their lines at *The Rocky Horror Picture Show,* thrashing around on the floor at standing-room-only punk shows in Baltimore and DC, protesting the arms race, marching to support AIDS research, writing letters for Amnesty International…

At least, Grey was wild. I was mostly a naive girl bent on protesting any injustice I could find, and utterly enamored of my punk-rock, rebel-with-a-cause boyfriend-fiancé-husband. It was only a few years into our marriage that I realized he wasn't really much of a rebel at all—just someone with a fierce disrespect for the powerful.

Heidi shrugs and glances over her shoulder, then cuts into the left lane and merges onto another road. "Well, you never know. And anyway, you've got till Sunday, so live a little. Break your curfew just this once. Plus, we're not eating there. I'm not dealing with parking near Fenway the night of a game against the Yankees. So we're meeting a couple of my friends at this great Vietnamese place, and we'll walk over to Fenway afterwards."

My shirt is riding up in the back. I tug down the hem and make a mental note to get a larger size tonight.

"I don't have a curfew." And I don't want to meet a bunch of other people, but I don't say so. Heidi is that friend who always pulls me from my comfort zone, and never asks me to admit she was right.

She doesn't respond except with a glance.

"Okay, fine. I have a curfew, but it's self-imposed." Grey lives in Baltimore, and even though he's been pretty involved until recently, I've always felt like I need to set a good example for Cal. As far as I can tell, it's worked—he lets me know where he's going, texts when he's going to be late… he's pretty damn responsible, as much as he's also an almost-eighteen-year-old boy.

"How is Cal?" Heidi asks. The unspoken question is, *Is Grey keeping his promises?* Heidi was my maid of honor, and the one person who knew I was leaving Grey even before I did. For now, I answer the spoken question.

"Cal is… he's good. He's spending the weekend at his friend Tim's. And speaking of making contributions to the world, he's thinking pre-law. He's applying to Jefferson University."

"Damn. Good for him…and good for you. Are you going to be okay on your own again WILL YOU FUCKING DRIVE OR MERGE ALREADY FUCKWAD next year?"

"Haven't I been on my own for ten years?"

"It's not the same, and you know it. If you were on your own, you'd have stood up for yourself at work years ago—or changed jobs."

On cue, my phone buzzes from the recesses of my purse. I ignore it.

Heidi pulls into a left turn lane I'm not sure we'll ever escape from, given that there's literally a train stopped across the intersection we need to turn into.

"I want to cover school for Cal—at least, his four-year degree. I know Grey has money set aside in some fund or other, but he's been acting weird the past few weeks and I'm not sure what's going on. I have to be ready for anything. Besides, I can't just quit—I'm not twenty anymore."

"That is exactly my point, Tracey—you're not twenty anymore. Why are you still working for someone who doesn't value you? If you want to work for non-profits, that's cool. Do what fulfills you. But you're way past dues-paying."

The train moves. Heidi follows the cars ahead of us through the intersection, onto a smaller street lined by both shops and dwellings. She's right, but I can't see a way out—not when I'm so beat by the time I get home, that I don't have the energy to pull my resume together. I can't imagine taking time off for interviews. And though Heidi means well—and is totally, one-hundred-percent correct—her barrage of straight-talk is more than I want, right now.

I sigh. "I know… but I thought you wanted me to relax and forget my everyday worries for a few days. Can't I at least enjoy the concert tonight before I start thinking about attaining personal fulfillment in my professional life?"

"Okay," she says, maneuvering into a spot on another wide street with a train running up the middle of it. "We'll table it, for now… but I think you shouldn't leave without a plan. Consider it part of clearing your head."

While Heidi pays for parking on her phone, I pull out my own phone, which is still buzzing insistently.

There's a notification badge on my Slack app, but I put off dealing with it to text Cal instead.

> MOM: Want me to pick up a concert tee for you?

The text goes unread, but he and Tim are probably out at a movie or somewhere with the rest of their friends. Maybe I'll just get him the shirt—if he doesn't want it, I'll have two. I'll use my rusty but still serviceable sewing skills to convert the extra one into a shopping bag… or, I could, if I had any spare time.

How did I let myself get trapped like this? How did I let myself turn into a workaholic—the very thing that pushed me to leave Grey? At least Grey got something out of his embrace of the job—he made partner at his law firm and can take all the pro-bono cases he wants. There's no room for me to either advance or grow at CAN. Damn Heidi for seeing it so plainly! And damn myself, for needing this meager vacation to call attention to how much my job takes out of me.

For several blocks, Heidi leads the way past multiple banks and a variety of eateries that aren't phở places, then angles us towards a little restaurant with a blue awning.

We enter a cramped but sensible vestibule with a fish tank housing a goldfish that's so large I wonder if it's really a koi. Before I can register anything beyond that, Heidi grabs my hand and tugs me into the restaurant after her, pausing at the hostess stand and scanning the tables. She leads me to the right, away from the bar and beneath a faux bamboo archway, to the front dining room. I push my mid-life crisis aside and brighten my expression as we approach a table already occupied by two. Along the way, we pass a couple on what is clearly a first date that's going awkwardly, an eclectic group of seven who are introducing themselves to each other, a mismatched-looking group of two guys and a girl with a disappointed air about her, and a frazzled-looking woman with an excited-looking teenager.

Heidi's friends, Sarah the dog groomer and David, the head of the sculpture department at a tiny art college, are side-by-side in one of the booths along the far wall. They're dressed in ball caps and replica jerseys, like they're on their way to the Red Sox game.

Seeing me eye their game-day gear, David flips his hat backwards, frat-boy-style, and says, "Heidi mentioned the concert a few days ago. I thought, since the House of Blues is right behind the ballpark, we should meet for dinner and all walk over to Fenway together."

He must be a Sox fan the way Grey is an Orioles fan. Worse, he has an easygoing smile and warm brown eyes like Grey does. He's probably tall, too. Never let it be said I don't have a type.

Heidi and I slide into the other side of the booth and peruse the menu briefly. It doesn't take long for me to zero in on a bowl of phở gà.

"So you've been friends since college?" Sarah asks, after we've all ordered.

I nod. "We actually met freshman year, in line before a Styrofoam Rockets show at the 9:30 Club in DC."

She laughs. "That's me and David. We were both—separately—looking for a ticket outside the stadium for a game against the Yankees, and we wound up sitting next to each other. So now we meet up for a couple games each season."

Oh, so they're not together?

I must have some idiotic look on my face, because Heidi kicks me under the table. Or maybe that frazzled woman bumped me—she's crawling around on the floor with a college student from one of the other tables, looking for something.

Either way, I don't know what I'm thinking, ogling David: I already have a life in DC and no time to date locally, never mind long-distance—as my still-buzzing phone reminds me. Just in case it's Cal texting me (even though I know it won't be), I pull my phone out.

"Sorry," I say. "There's a new guy at this conference center we work with, and he's a pain in the..." I pause, too used to not cussing in front of others. It's one more curse of being a single mom: I never got around to letting up on the behavioral changes I implemented when Cal was young.

"Ass?" David queries.

"Yeah," I say, and everyone laughs a little.

"I know the type," says David. "We have some students— and parents—at Salem College of Art who fit that bill."

I scan through the series of Slack messages—no longer just from Tod, but also Steven and Addison.

> **GROUP: STEVEN, ADDISON, TRACEY**
>
> STEVEN: Tracey I'm sorry for sending this, but Tod from the conference center is saying Old Potomac can't accommodate catering for the conference next month, even though they did so pre-pandemic, and even though it's part of the contract we negotiated with them in January when we reserved the space. Something about construction. Advice?
>
> ADDISON: Tracey, don't worry about it— enjoy your weekend. Steven and I will brainstorm some solutions tonight, and I'll send you our thoughts by email so you can weigh in once you're back on Monday.

Of course Addison jumped on this for me—and of course I'm fighting the urge to ask for more details than "some-thing about construction." I glance up, feeling utterly rude. "I'm so sorry. I've been getting messages all afternoon. It just figures, the first time in five years I take an actual weekend to myself, and everything goes to shit the minute I'm on the plane."

David passes me the plate of summer rolls. "Where do you work?"

I select a chilled, full-to-bursting roll and dollop a spoonful of the peanut sauce onto my plate. "I'm at a small, mid-Atlantic non-profit, Climate Action Now. I'm pretty much a Jane-of-All-Trades, there, though my background is in copywriting and editing."

"You must be indispensable," he jokes.

"You'd think so, the way my phone is blowing up," I reply. "But they'd be fine if I decided to throw in the towel and just follow the Styrofoam Rockets on tour."

"Is that a thing that people do, with the Styrofoam Rockets?" David asks. "What are their uber-dedicated fans even called?"

"Um... maybe... I might have... possibly... perhaps... tried to work something like that out as part of my misspent youth," I confess. Sarah laughs. Beside me, Heidi hides her face in her hands, in mock-embarrassment. Her nails are manicured (unlike mine) and adorned with red rockets. David has a half-smile on his face, as if he's unable to tell if I'm joking or not. "Maybe," I say, meeting his gaze, "I can tell you that story sometime. Life on the road as a Packing Peanut was quite an adventure."

My phone buzzes again, so I hold a finger up in that hang-on-a-sec gesture, then turn back to the Slack messages.

GROUP: TOD, STEVEN, ADDISON,
TRACEY

> TOD: Sharing here per Steven's request.
> Old Potomac no longer provides catering
> as a service for conferences. That will need
> to be arranged separately by an outside
> vendor. Access to our kitchen facility is not
> guaranteed. The policy went into effect
> August of this year.

> STEVEN: I still don't understand why we
> weren't notified of this change before it was
> implemented, and more importantly, why
> our existing contract will not be honored.
> We've held our annual conference at Old
> Potomac for years, and at this late date we
> cannot be certain of finding a caterer who
> can commit to our event dates, let alone
> work without access to your kitchen.

> TOD: As I've explained several times today,
> this is a new policy, and it is firm. My hands
> are tied and I'm unable to make exceptions
> to existing contract-holders. Our kitchen
> facility is under renovation and based on
> our contractor's schedule, we will have no
> running water. Tracey, I suggest you and I
> talk tomorrow to make sure we are both on
> the same page, as your event date is
> approaching rapidly.

No running water? I'm supposed to find a caterer, at the eleventh hour, that can operate without running water?

From a nearby table, over the commotion of the girl still carrying on about whatever she lost, a woman shouts, "He's choking! Somebody help him!"

It's an older couple. The man's face is red and there's a look of terror on his face as he struggles for air that won't come.

A busboy with bright pink hair rushes over to the choking man. "I am going to help you!" he shouts, then positions himself behind the man. After a few good thrusts, a piece of chewed-up food flies out of the man's mouth and his color returns to normal.

My phone has been buzzing this whole time, so I tear my attention from the scene around me.

> GROUP: TOD, STEVEN, ADDISON, TRACEY
>
> TOD: Tracey?
>
> TOD: Tracey? Let's meet tomorrow.
>
> TOD: Tracey, I need a response.
>
> TOD: Ok, then, I'm scheduling time at eight tomorrow. You can meet me at Old Potomac.

This is fucking absurd. I'm going to have to end this now or it's going to drag on all night.

> GROUP: TOD, STEVEN, ADDISON, TRACEY
>
> TRACEY: I can't deal with this right now, and I won't meet tomorrow. Neither will Steven or Addison, as they'll be reaching out to our lawyer about your breach of contract.

> TRACEY: Tod, Old Potomac's renovation schedule is not our problem. You will honor the existing contract with Climate Action Now, or you'll answer to our lawyer (see above).

> TRACEY: I AM ON VACATION.

I look up again and meet David's eyes. He's got the beginnings of laugh lines around them. My heart fluttering absurdly, I take a deep breath, and delete the Slack app from my phone. My gut lurches a little.

It's just for the weekend, but I need to be present where I am, for a change. I *want* to be. I smile at David. He smiles back.

Contributors' Bios

Mina Allan

Mina Allan writes cozy mysteries and plots dastardly deeds from her home in Massachusetts. She loves a fruity cocktail and is always in search of the perfect purse. Mina also happens to be the alter-ego of Table for 7 co-founder Erin Dionne. Find her on IG at @mina_allan.books.

G. J. Crespo

Leaving dastardly and dark to his fellow group members, Gary writes relationship fiction for YA and adults in his sunny home office north of Boston. Gary misses in-person meetings with his group, not just for the great food, but because it's nearly impossible to deliver a good stink-eye over Zoom. Find him at www.tablefor7press.com/g-j-crespo.

Wendy M. McDonald

When not penning mostly-darkish stories in the garret of her New England home, Wendy knits socks, argues with her beagle, and generally acts like a dork. Recent reports indicate Wendy is an unstoppable force fueled by Diet Coke, potato chips, and unmitigated tenacity. Find her at wendymmcdonald.com and on IG at @wmmcdonald.

Megan M. Mullin

Travel writer by day, urban fantasy writer by night—Megan is always ready for an adventure (though her budget says otherwise). Likes include the ocean, Pop Tarts, clean sheets, and discovering new places. Megan can usually be found in her Boston home, singing personalized songs to her rescue dog, Teddy. She can also be found on IG @meganmmullin.

Phoebe Sinclair

Phoebe Sinclair is a writer / wanderer / friend. She writes lyrical contemporary fiction featuring young people of color. She 'daylights' at two non-profits, moonlights as founding member of a cool indie publishing collective, and honestly loves candy corn. Find her at: phoebesinclair-writes.com and on ex-Twitter and IG at @wholeheartlocal.

Annette Trossello

When she's not teaching kindergarten through fifth graders library media, you can find Annette Trossello working on her screenplay about the people we lose, the walls we build, and who's worth breaking them down for. She also enjoys playing games with her family, stand up paddle boarding, and reading. Find her at https://www.tablefor7press.com/about-us.

About Table for 7 Press

We are an independent publishing collective—by writers, for writers.

We believe in supportive, clear communication about the work that we create, and feedback that is instructive and honest. Prior to March 2020, we met bi-weekly in restaurants near Coolidge Corner and Fenway Park, and occasionally at the Writers' Loft in Hudson, Massachusetts. These days, like many others, we meet online.

It was late one evening, as our online meeting wound down and we commiserated over our longing for a scoop of frozen satisfaction from J.P. Licks, that we realized how perfectly our combined skill-set enabled us to circumvent the big publishing houses and put our voices out into the world. After the shock wore off, we agreed to support each other in this exciting new endeavor, and Table for 7 Press was born!

Connect with us online at www.tablefor7press.com and on social media.

facebook.com/Tablefor7Press

x.com/tablefor7press

instagram.com/tablefor7press

Also from Table for 7 Press

A Parade & A Perp by Mina Alan

How to Ruin Your Life in 140 Characters or Less by G. J. Crespo

Bad Choices Make Good Stories by Erin M. Dionne

The Willow by Wendy M. McDonald